The Story of
SHERLOCK HOLMES
The Famous Detective

Sherlock Holmes and his helpful friend Dr. John Watson are fictional characters created by British writer Sir Arthur Conan Doyle. Doyle published his first novel about the pair, *A Study in Scarlet*, in 1887, and it became very successful. Doyle went on to write fif[ty]... ... ..., as well as three more nove... ... ... *Sign of Four* (189... ...tures—*The* ... ...askervilles (1902), and *The Val*... ...

Sherlock Holmes ... Dr. Watson have become some of the most famous book characters of all time. Holmes spent most of his time solving mysteries, but he also had a wide array of hobbies, such as playing the violin, boxing, and sword fighting. Watson, a retired army doctor, met Holmes through a mutual friend when Holmes was looking for a roommate. Watson lived with Holmes for several years at 221B Baker Street before marrying and moving out. However, after his marriage, Watson continued to assist Holmes with his cases.

The original versions of the Sherlock Holmes stories are still printed, and many have been made into movies and television shows. Readers continue to be impressed by Holmes's detective methods of observation and scientific reason.

#1

ON the CASE with
HOLMES and WATSON

SHERLOCK HOLMES

and a Scandal in Bohemia

Based on the stories of
Sir Arthur Conan Doyle

Adapted by **Murray Shaw** and **M. J. Cosson**
Illustrated by **Sophie Rohrbach**

GRAPHIC UNIVERSE™ • MINNEAPOLIS • NEW YORK • LONDON

Grateful acknowledgment to Dame Jean Conan Doyle for permission to use the Sherlock Holmes characters created by Sir Arthur Conan Doyle

Graphic Universe™
A division of Lerner Publishing Group, Inc.
241 First Avenue North
Minneapolis, MN 55401 U.S.A.

Website address: www.lernerbooks.com

Library of Congress Cataloging-in-Publication Data

Shaw, Murray.
    #1 Sherlock Holmes and a scandal in Bohemia / adapted by Murray Shaw and M.J. Cosson ; illustrated by Sophie Rohrbach ; from the original stories by Sir Arthur Conan Doyle.
       p.   cm. — (On the case with Holmes and Watson)
    Summary: Retold in graphic novel form, Sherlock Holmes attempts to retrieve a photograph being used to blackmail the King of Bohemia and finds something even more valuable. Includes a section explaining Holmes's reasoning and the clues he used to solve the mystery.
       ISBN 978-0-7613-6185-5 (lib. bdg. : alk. paper)
       1. Graphic novels. (1. Graphic novels. 2. Doyle, Arthur Conan, Sir, 1859–1930. Scandal in Bohemia—Adaptations. 3. Mystery and detective stories.) I. Cosson, M. J. II. Rohrbach, Sophie, ill. III. Doyle, Arthur Conan, Sir, 1859–1930. Scandal in Bohemia. IV. Title. V. Title: Scandal in Bohemia.
    PZ7.7.S46She 2011
    741.5'973—dc22
                                                                    2009051763

Manufactured in the United States of America
3—BC—9/1/11

Character List

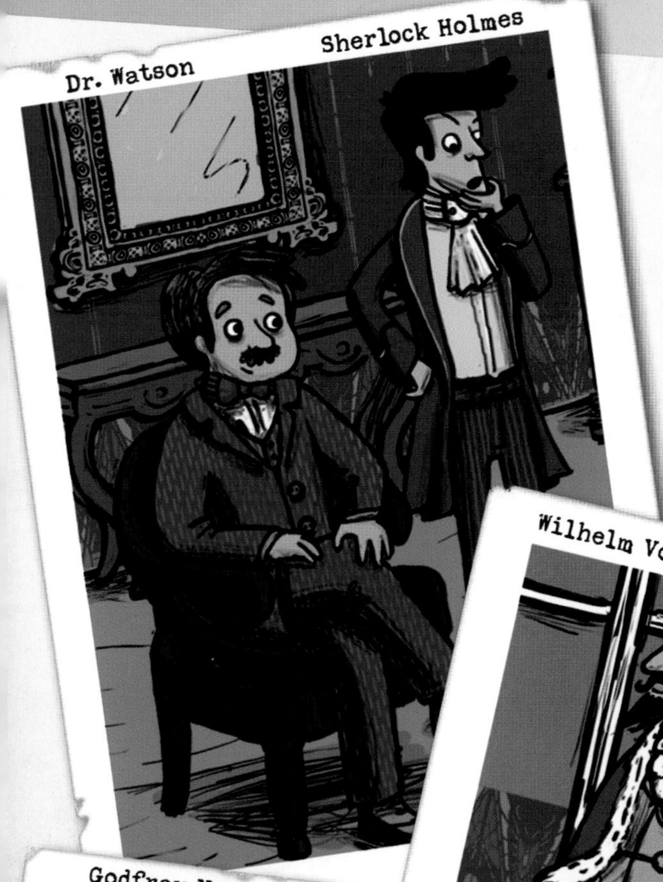
Dr. Watson
Sherlock Holmes

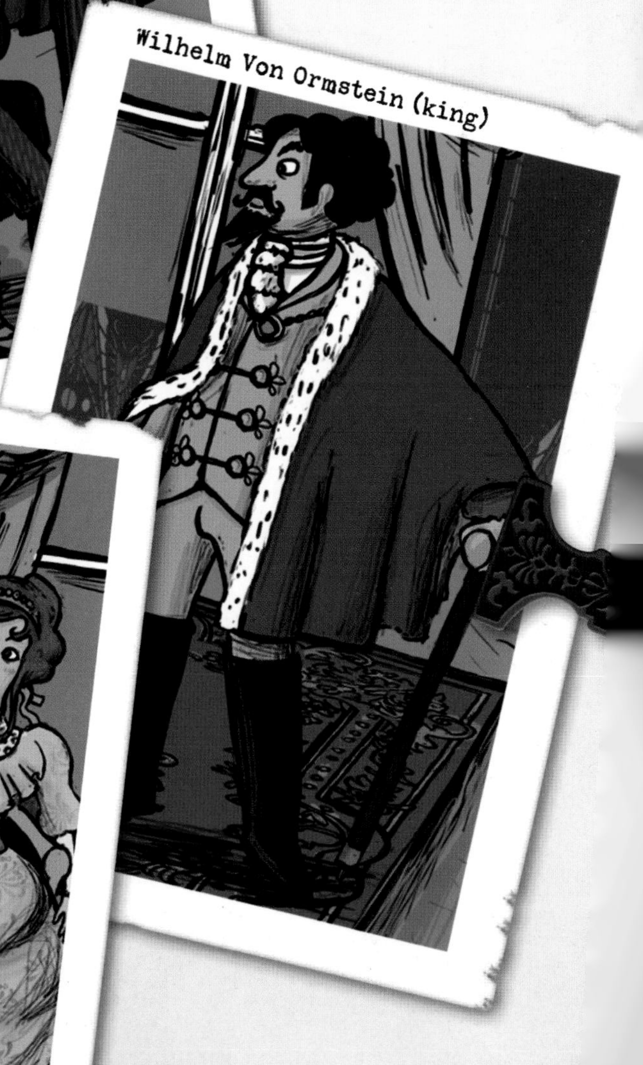
Wilhelm Von Ormstein (king)

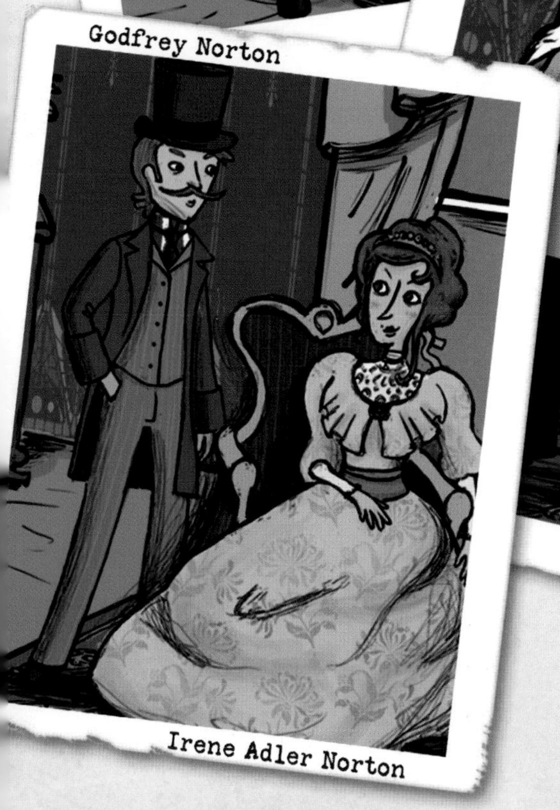
Godfrey Norton
Irene Adler Norton

From the Desk of
John H. Watson, M.D.

My name is Dr. John H. Watson. For several years, I have been assisting my friend, Sherlock Holmes, in solving mysteries throughout the bustling city of London and beyond. Holmes is a peculiar man—always questioning and reasoning his way through various problems. But when I first met him in 1878, I was immediately intrigued by his oddities.

Holmes has always been more daring than I, and his logical deduction never ceases to amaze me. I have begun writing down all of the adventures I have with Holmes. This is one of those stories.

Sincerely,

Dr. Watson

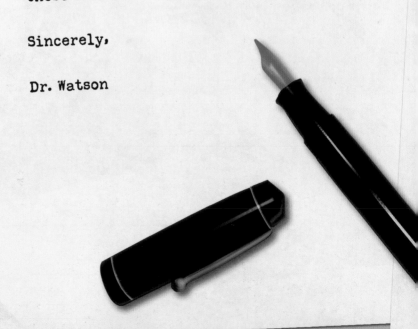

As he spoke, we both heard the sound of horse's hooves and carriage wheels outside. We went to the window and looked down to see an ornate carriage and two handsome horses waiting at the curb below. There would be money in this case! A moment later, there was a knock on the door.

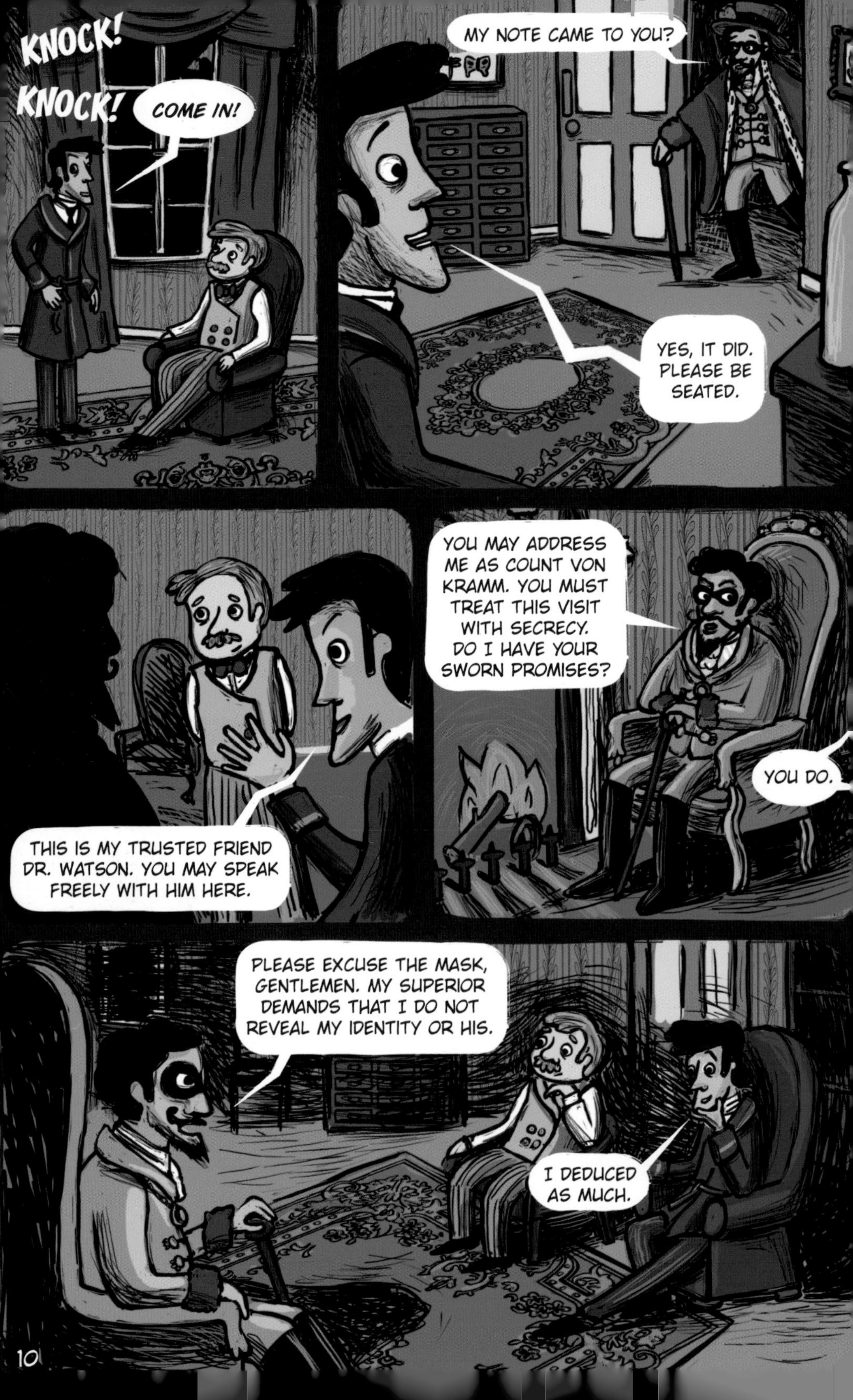
KNOCK!
KNOCK!
COME IN!
MY NOTE CAME TO YOU?
YES, IT DID. PLEASE BE SEATED.
THIS IS MY TRUSTED FRIEND DR. WATSON. YOU MAY SPEAK FREELY WITH HIM HERE.
YOU MAY ADDRESS ME AS COUNT VON KRAMM. YOU MUST TREAT THIS VISIT WITH SECRECY. DO I HAVE YOUR SWORN PROMISES?
YOU DO.
PLEASE EXCUSE THE MASK, GENTLEMEN. MY SUPERIOR DEMANDS THAT I DO NOT REVEAL MY IDENTITY OR HIS.
I DEDUCED AS MUCH.

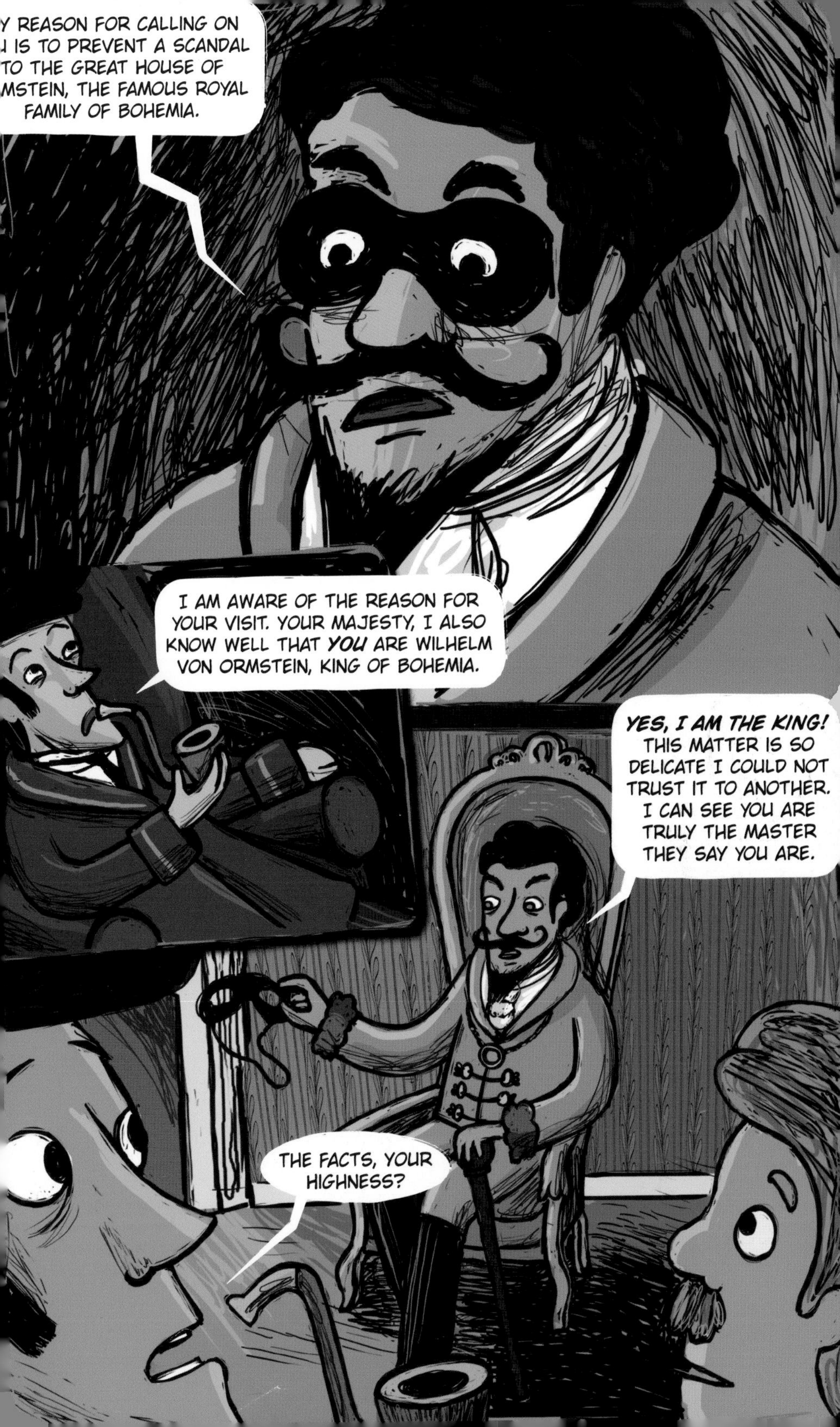
Y REASON FOR CALLING ON
I IS TO PREVENT A SCANDAL
TO THE GREAT HOUSE OF
MSTEIN, THE FAMOUS ROYAL
FAMILY OF BOHEMIA.
I AM AWARE OF THE REASON FOR YOUR VISIT. YOUR MAJESTY, I ALSO KNOW WELL THAT *YOU* ARE WILHELM VON ORMSTEIN, KING OF BOHEMIA.
YES, I AM THE KING! THIS MATTER IS SO DELICATE I COULD NOT TRUST IT TO ANOTHER. I CAN SEE YOU ARE TRULY THE MASTER THEY SAY YOU ARE.
THE FACTS, YOUR HIGHNESS?

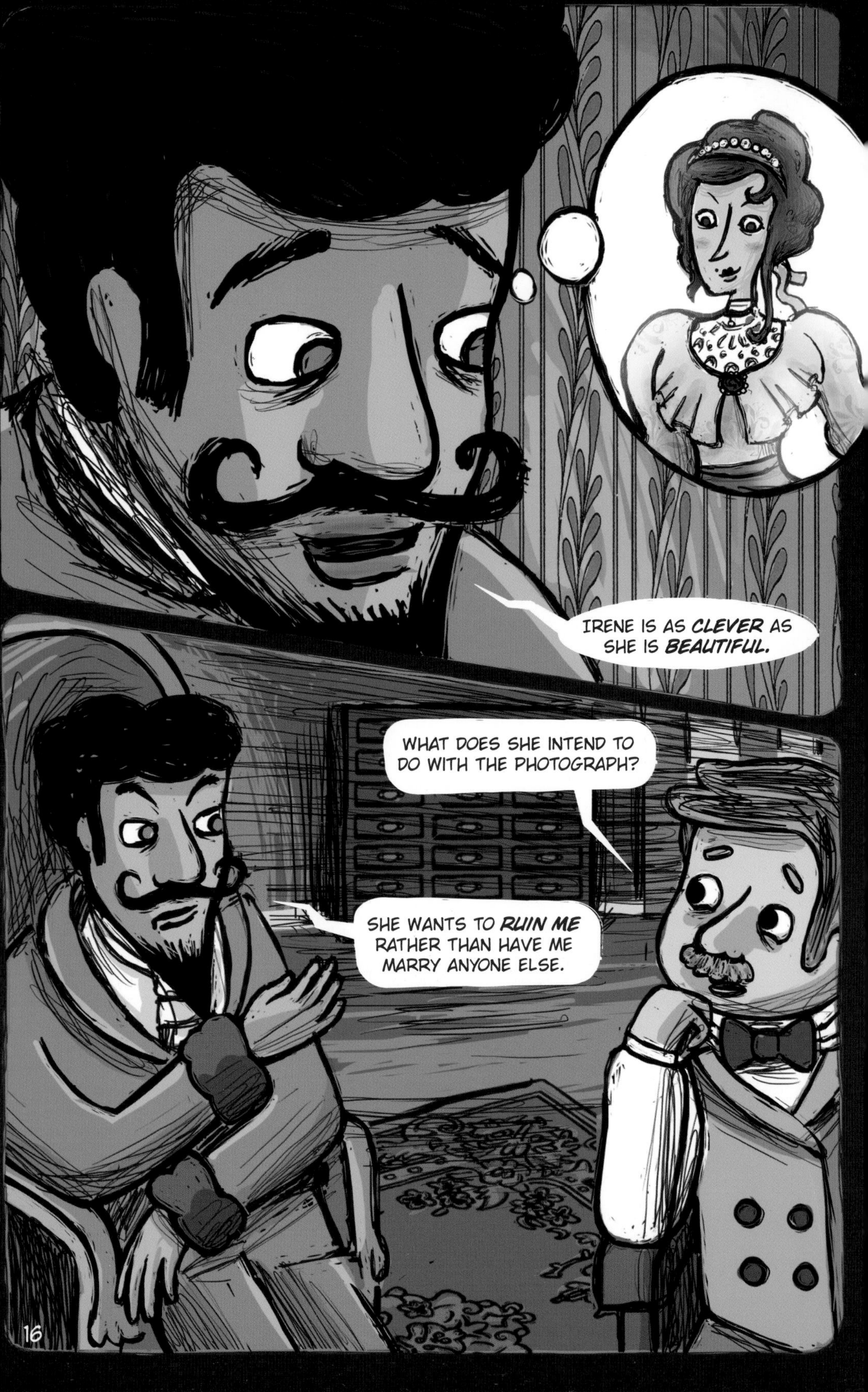
IRENE IS AS *CLEVER* AS SHE IS *BEAUTIFUL.*
WHAT DOES SHE INTEND TO DO WITH THE PHOTOGRAPH?
SHE WANTS TO *RUIN ME* RATHER THAN HAVE ME MARRY ANYONE ELSE.

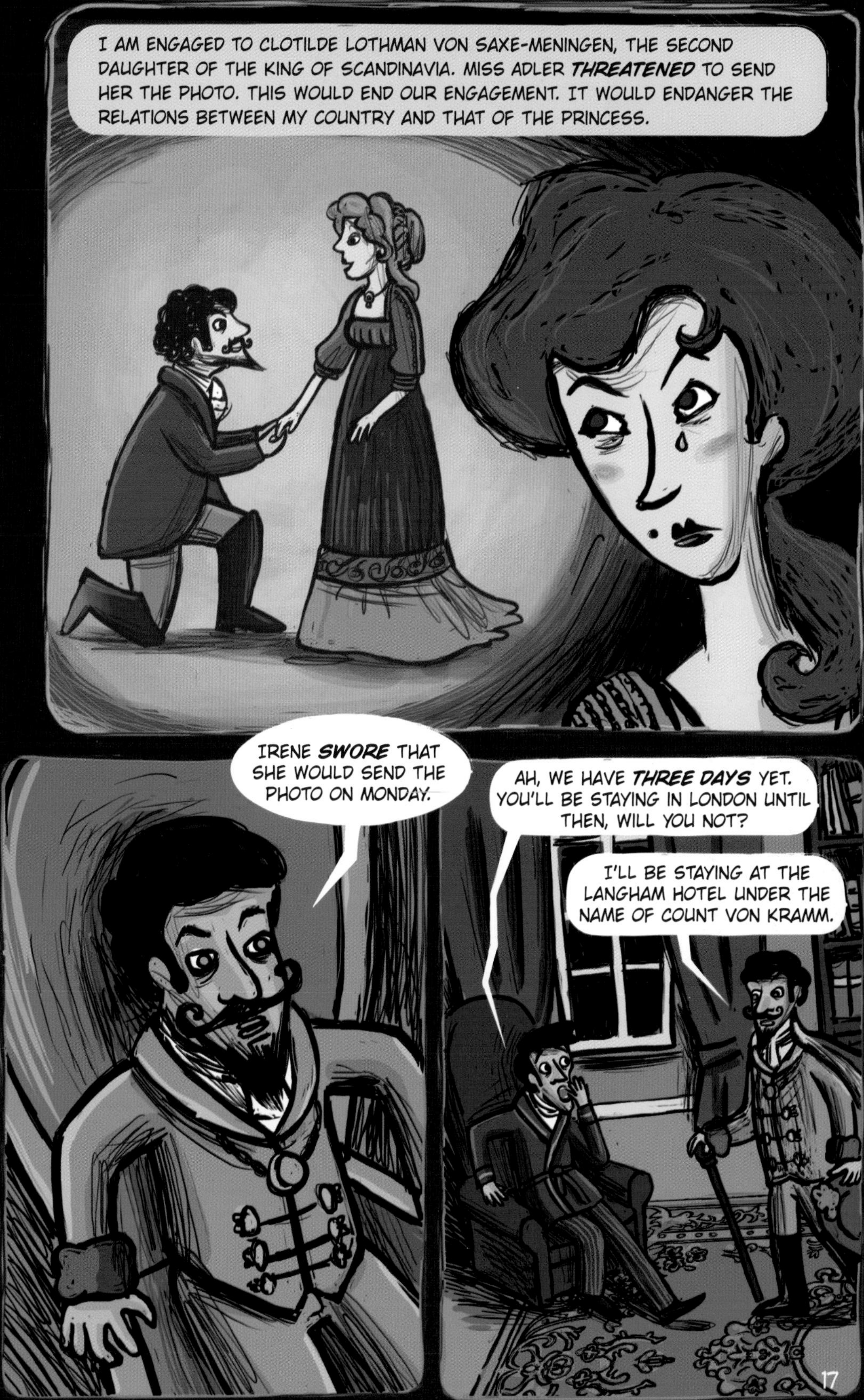

I AM ENGAGED TO CLOTILDE LOTHMAN VON SAXE-MENINGEN, THE SECOND DAUGHTER OF THE KING OF SCANDINAVIA. MISS ADLER *THREATENED* TO SEND HER THE PHOTO. THIS WOULD END OUR ENGAGEMENT. IT WOULD ENDANGER THE RELATIONS BETWEEN MY COUNTRY AND THAT OF THE PRINCESS.
IRENE *SWORE* THAT SHE WOULD SEND THE PHOTO ON MONDAY.
AH, WE HAVE *THREE DAYS* YET. YOU'LL BE STAYING IN LONDON UNTIL THEN, WILL YOU NOT?
I'LL BE STAYING AT THE LANGHAM HOTEL UNDER THE NAME OF COUNT VON KRAMM.

March 24, 1888, 3:00 p.m.

Holmes requested my assistance for this unusual case. Of course, I agreed to help, excited at the prospect of yet another adventure with him. Holmes asked me to return to his apartment the next day at three o'clock.

I returned to the Baker Street lodging promptly at three, but Holmes was not there. Unsure of his whereabouts, I decided to wait. At about four o'clock, I heard someone stumbling on the steps.

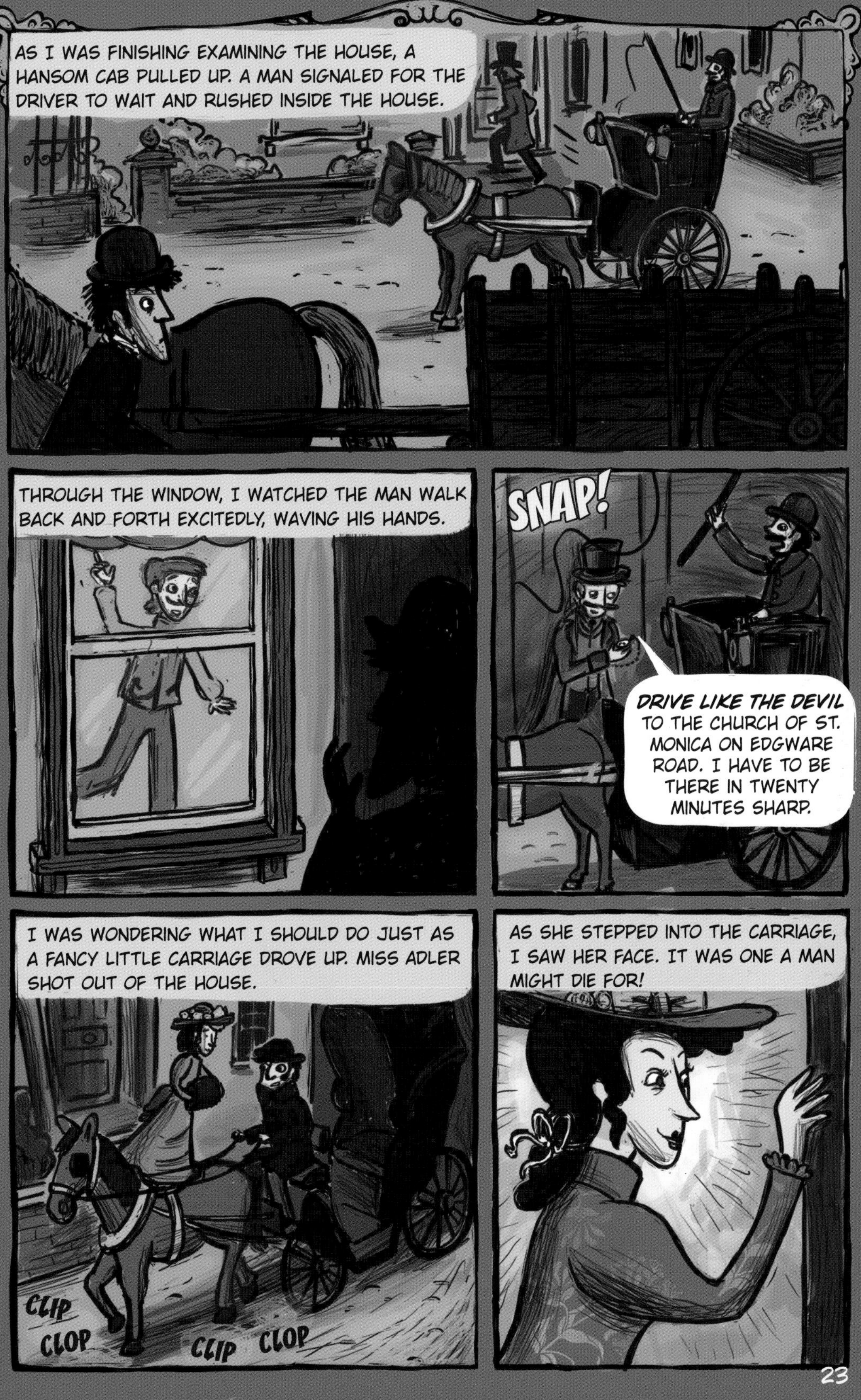
AS I WAS FINISHING EXAMINING THE HOUSE, A HANSOM CAB PULLED UP. A MAN SIGNALED FOR THE DRIVER TO WAIT AND RUSHED INSIDE THE HOUSE.
THROUGH THE WINDOW, I WATCHED THE MAN WALK BACK AND FORTH EXCITEDLY, WAVING HIS HANDS.
SNAP!
DRIVE LIKE THE DEVIL TO THE CHURCH OF ST. MONICA ON EDGWARE ROAD. I HAVE TO BE THERE IN TWENTY MINUTES SHARP.
I WAS WONDERING WHAT I SHOULD DO JUST AS A FANCY LITTLE CARRIAGE DROVE UP. MISS ADLER SHOT OUT OF THE HOUSE.
CLIP CLOP CLIP CLOP
AS SHE STEPPED INTO THE CARRIAGE, I SAW HER FACE. IT WAS ONE A MAN MIGHT DIE FOR!

Holmes's last sentence and excited voice were certainly unexpected. Never before had his cool-headed reasoning allowed him to comment on a woman's charms. From this I deduced that Irene Adler must indeed be an exceptional lady. Holmes continued telling his story at a rapid pace . . .

Holmes went into his bedroom and soon returned looking like a gentle, simple-minded country clergyman. A broadcloth hat, baggy trousers, white tie, and worn black coat had transformed the Holmes I knew. He peered at me through small wire spectacles and piously folded his hands. I had to laugh. The stage had lost a fine actor when Holmes turned his talents to solving crime. It was time to make our way to the lady's house.

Just then a carriage approached the lodge. As the carriage slowed, several guardsmen rushed to open the door for the woman inside, in hopes of earning a coin or two. I watched as one shoved another, and a fierce quarrel broke out. In an instant, the lady was in the midst of a group of angry men.

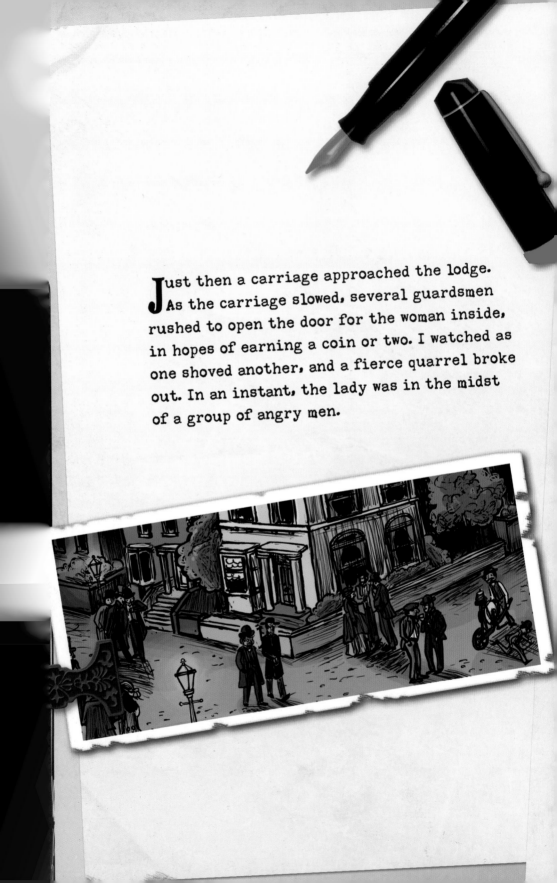

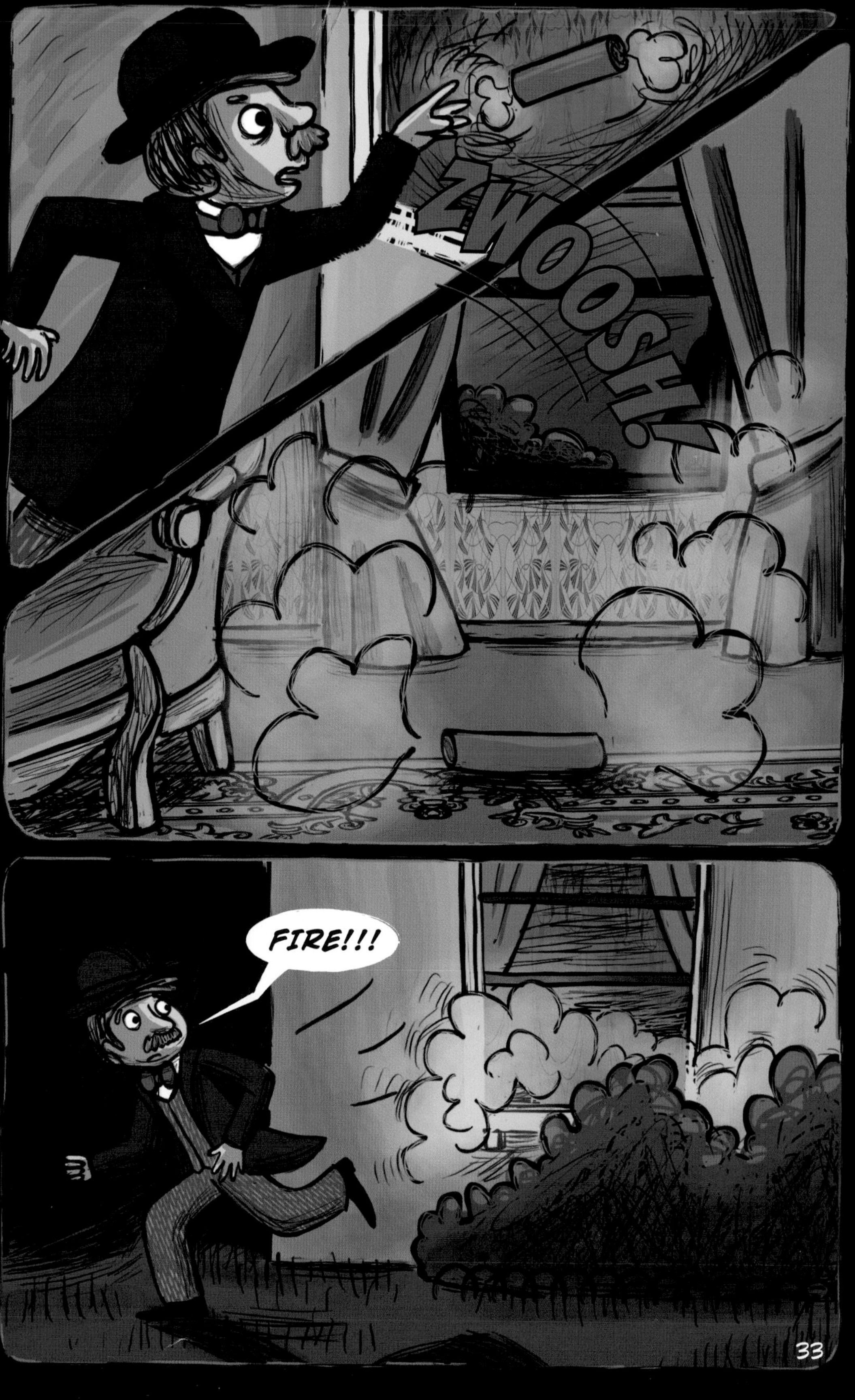
ZWOOSH!
FIRE!!!

Inside, people were rushing around until the maid found the bomb and yelled out "false alarm." I slipped away to the street corner, where I was soon joined by the disguised Holmes. We walked swiftly down Serpentine Avenue without talking until we reached the quieter streets of Edgware Road. I was dying to know if he had discovered the photograph.

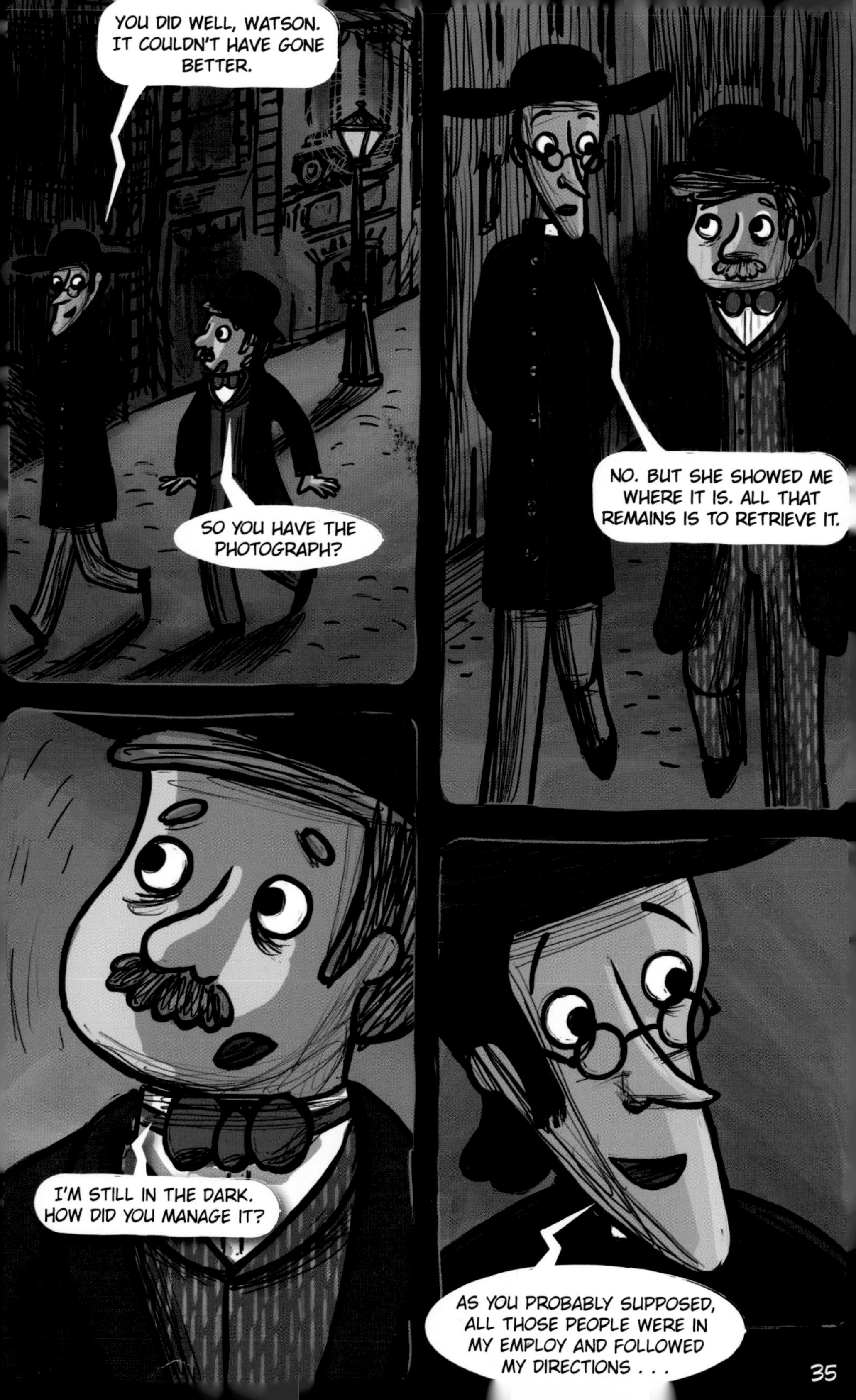
YOU DID WELL, WATSON. IT COULDN'T HAVE GONE BETTER.
SO YOU HAVE THE PHOTOGRAPH?
NO. BUT SHE SHOWED ME WHERE IT IS. ALL THAT REMAINS IS TO RETRIEVE IT.
I'M STILL IN THE DARK. HOW DID YOU MANAGE IT?
AS YOU PROBABLY SUPPOSED, ALL THOSE PEOPLE WERE IN MY EMPLOY AND FOLLOWED MY DIRECTIONS . . .

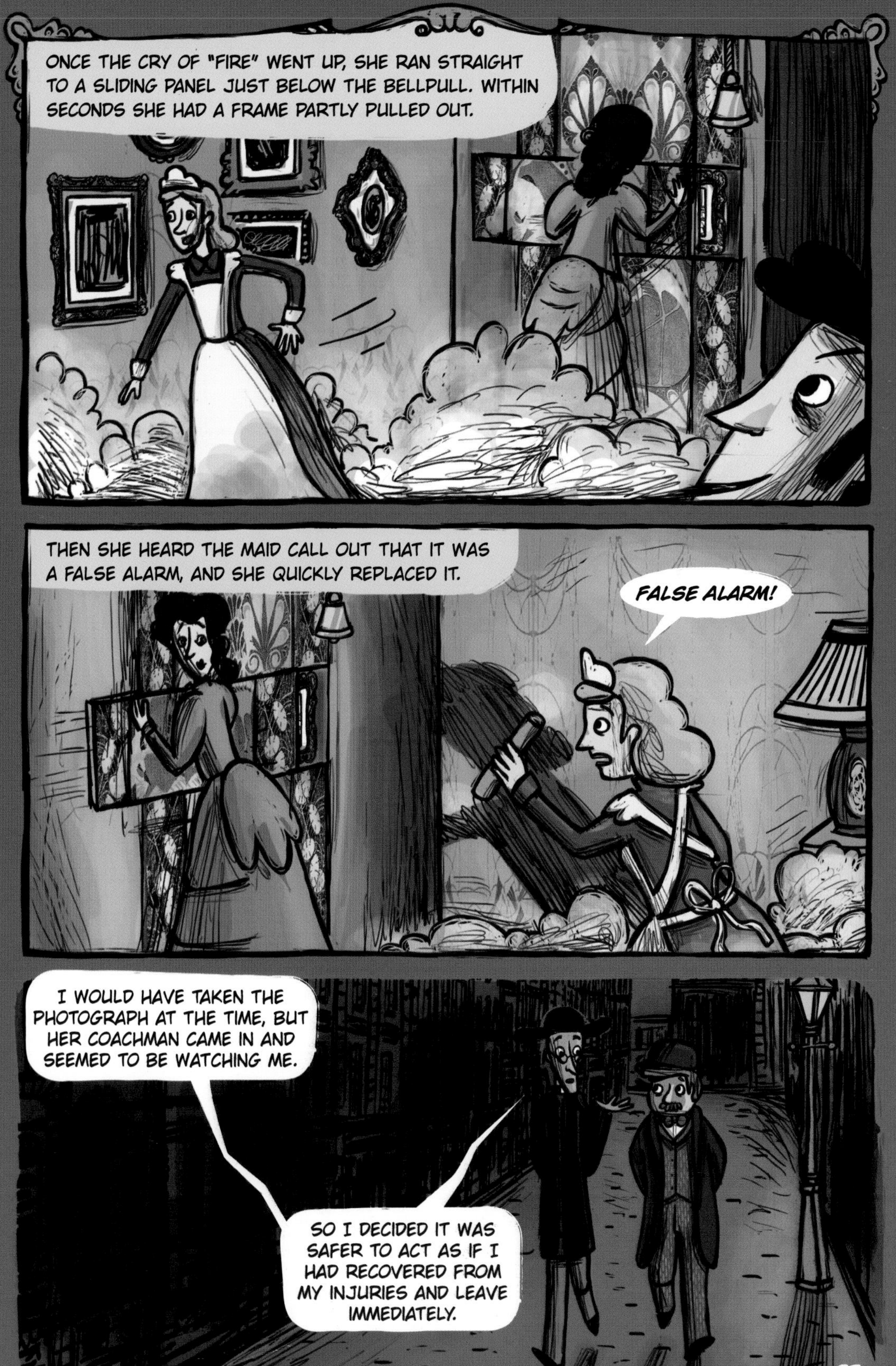
ONCE THE CRY OF "FIRE" WENT UP, SHE RAN STRAIGHT TO A SLIDING PANEL JUST BELOW THE BELLPULL. WITHIN SECONDS SHE HAD A FRAME PARTLY PULLED OUT.
THEN SHE HEARD THE MAID CALL OUT THAT IT WAS A FALSE ALARM, AND SHE QUICKLY REPLACED IT.
FALSE ALARM!
I WOULD HAVE TAKEN THE PHOTOGRAPH AT THE TIME, BUT HER COACHMAN CAME IN AND SEEMED TO BE WATCHING ME.
SO I DECIDED IT WAS SAFER TO ACT AS IF I HAD RECOVERED FROM MY INJURIES AND LEAVE IMMEDIATELY.

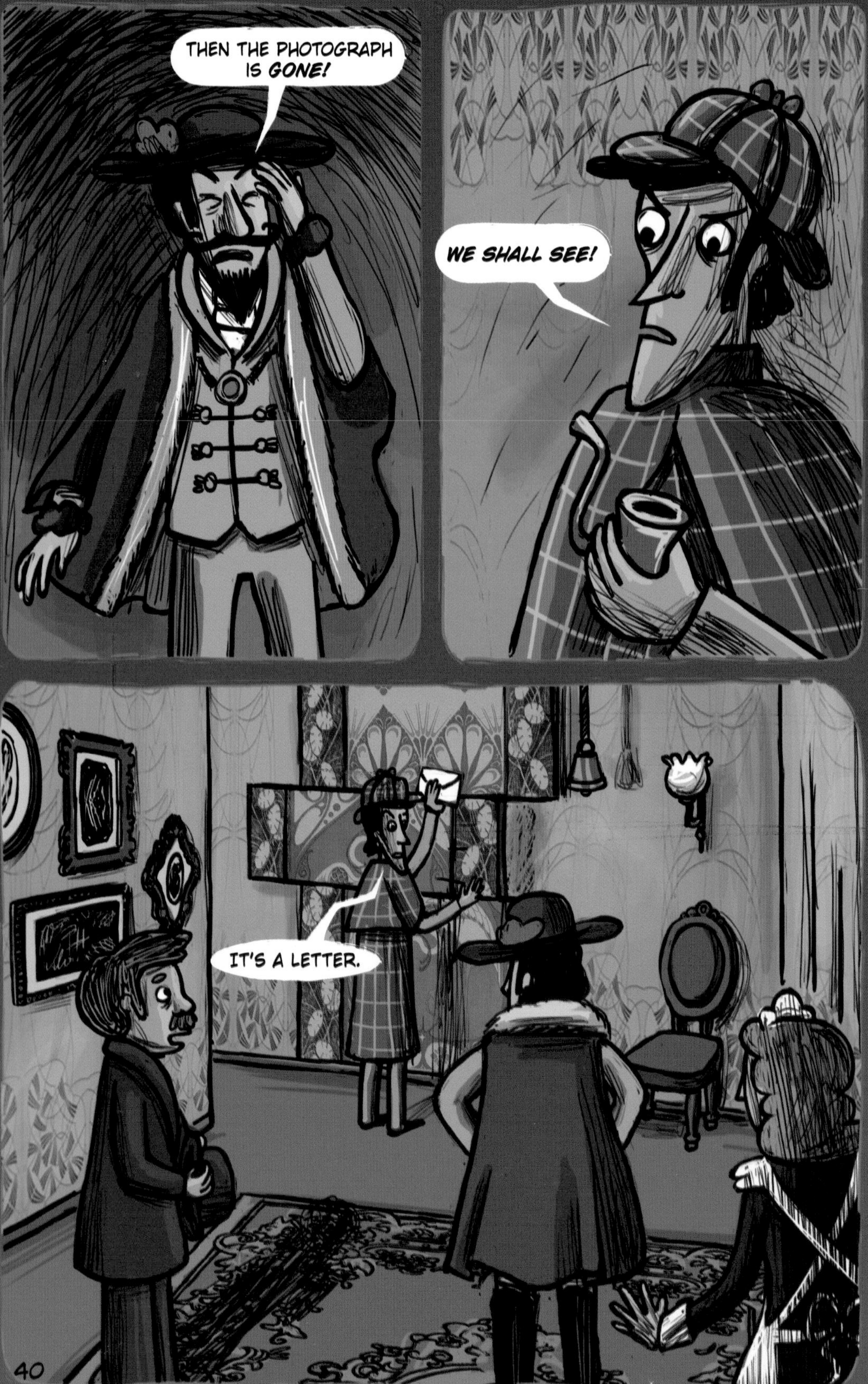
THEN THE PHOTOGRAPH IS *GONE!*
WE SHALL SEE!
IT'S A LETTER.

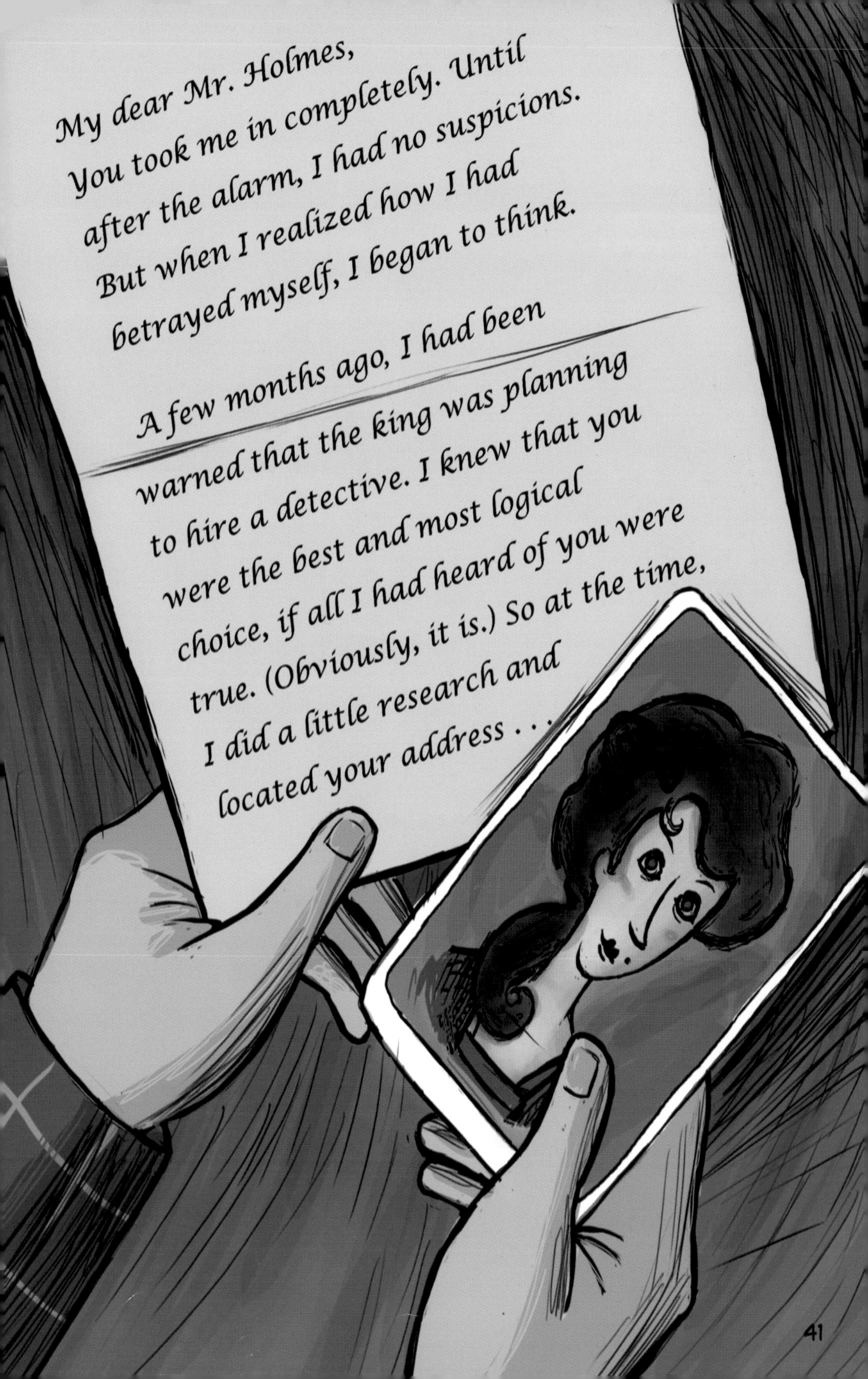
My dear Mr. Holmes,
You took me in completely. Until after the alarm, I had no suspicions. But when I realized how I had betrayed myself, I began to think.
A few months ago, I had been warned that the king was planning to hire a detective. I knew that you were the best and most logical choice, if all I had heard of you were true. (Obviously, it is.) So at the time, I did a little research and located your address . . .

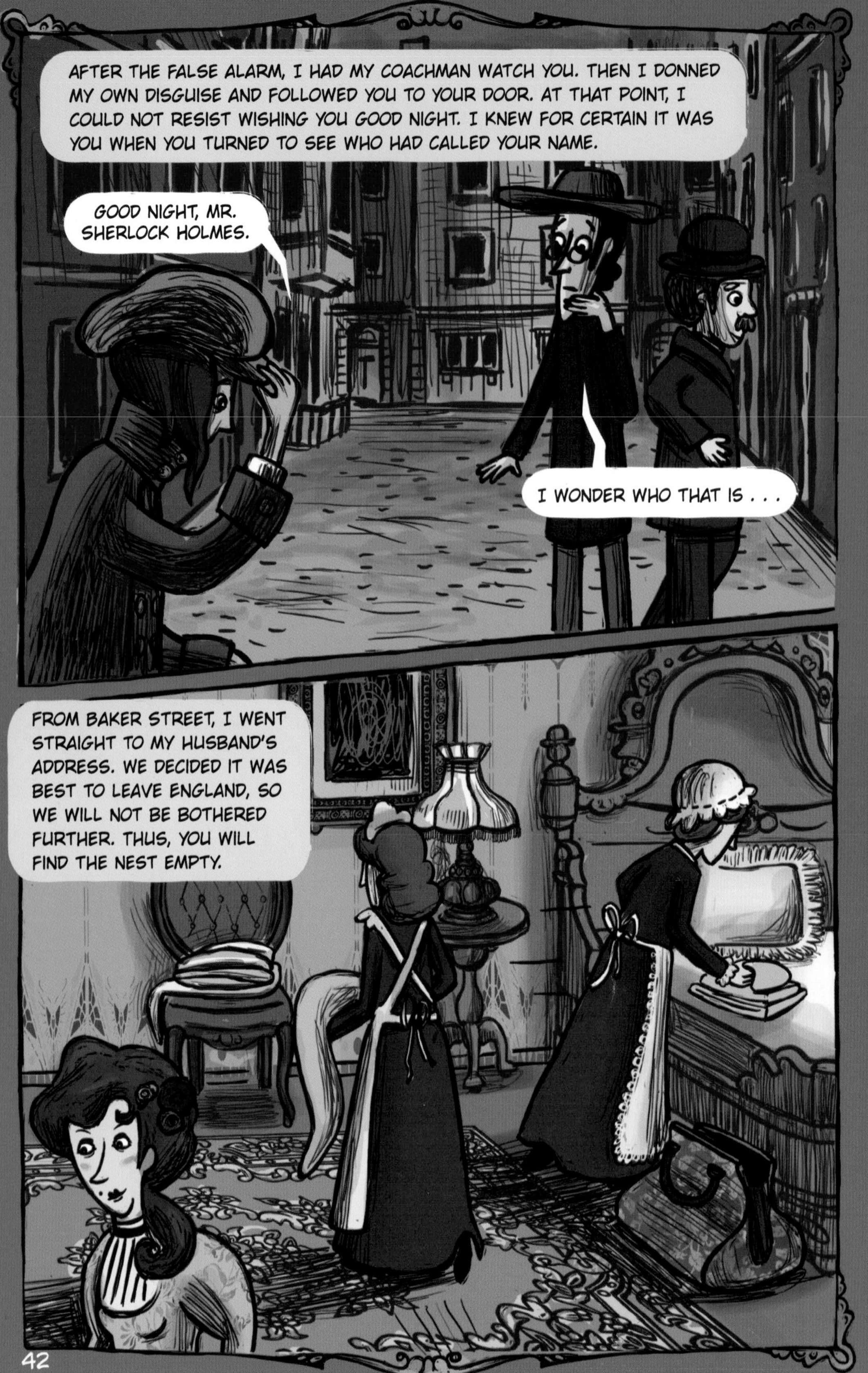
AFTER THE FALSE ALARM, I HAD MY COACHMAN WATCH YOU. THEN I DONNED MY OWN DISGUISE AND FOLLOWED YOU TO YOUR DOOR. AT THAT POINT, I COULD NOT RESIST WISHING YOU GOOD NIGHT. I KNEW FOR CERTAIN IT WAS YOU WHEN YOU TURNED TO SEE WHO HAD CALLED YOUR NAME.
GOOD NIGHT, MR. SHERLOCK HOLMES.
I WONDER WHO THAT IS . . .
FROM BAKER STREET, I WENT STRAIGHT TO MY HUSBAND'S ADDRESS. WE DECIDED IT WAS BEST TO LEAVE ENGLAND, SO WE WILL NOT BE BOTHERED FURTHER. THUS, YOU WILL FIND THE NEST EMPTY.

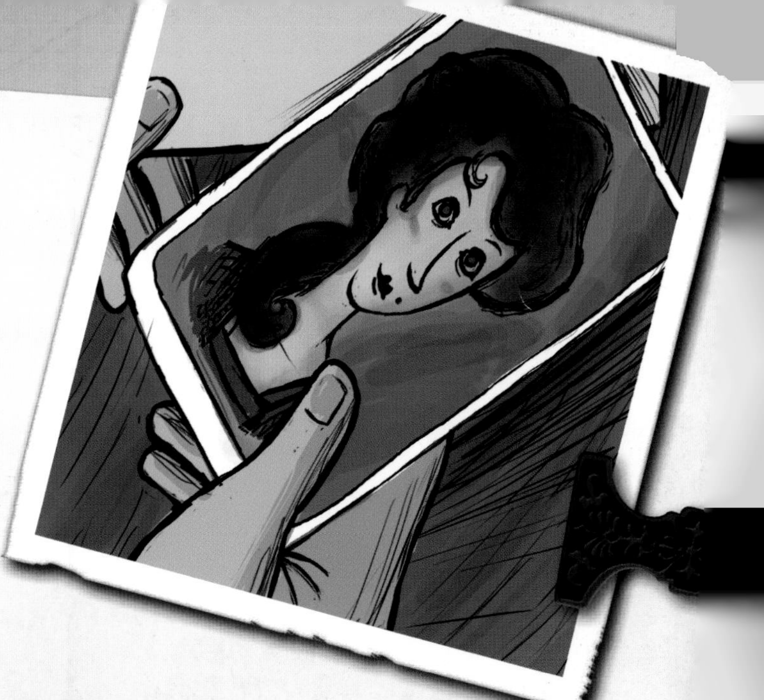

From that point on, Holmes never again referred to Irene Norton (née Adler) by her name. She has always been called, with the greatest honor—the woman. There has been no other for Holmes. She did what few could do—she outsmarted him.

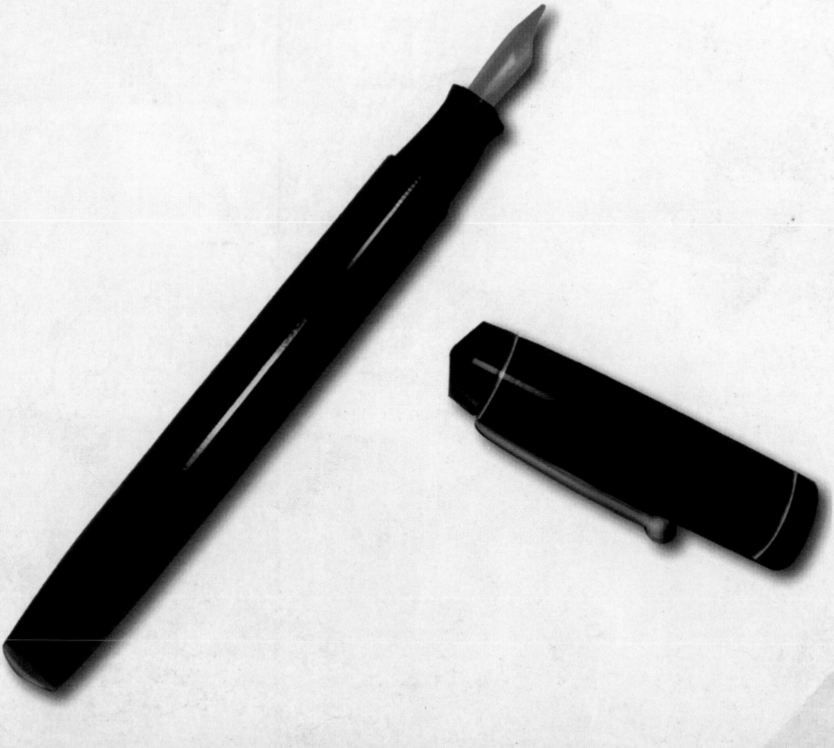

From the Desk of
John H. Watson, M.D.

A Scandal in Bohemia: How Did Holmes Solve It?

Why did Holmes suspect that Miss Adler kept the photograph in her sitting room?

From the attempts to rob her, Miss Adler knew people were looking for her photograph and letters. Holmes reasoned that she would hide them in a place where she could watch them and get a hold of them easily.

Why did Holmes stage a fight and dress as a clergyman?

BANG!
WHACK!

Miss Adler was known to be a strong-willed woman but one with a warm heart. Since burglary had failed, Holmes figured it would be better to appeal to the woman's kindness.

Why did Holmes fake a fire?

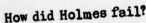

In the case of a fire, most people try to save their most valued possessions before fleeing the building. Holmes hoped that Miss Adler would reveal her hiding place as she left.

How did Holmes fail?

Holmes underestimated his opponent's awareness and intelligence. Because of Irene Adler's great respect for Holmes's capabilities, she suspected the fake fire was the work of the master detective. She, therefore, used her acting abilities and a disguise of her own to confirm her suspicions. Thus, Miss Adler became one of the few people ever to outsmart Sherlock Holmes.